Marks On A Page

Wade Kernohan

Marks On A Page

Wade Kernohan

Published by 1st World Publishing
P.O. Box 2211, Fairfield, Iowa 52556
tel: 641-209-5000 • fax: 866-440-5234
web: www.1stworldpublishing.com

First Edition

LCCN: 2013921703
ISBN: 978-1-4218-8680-0

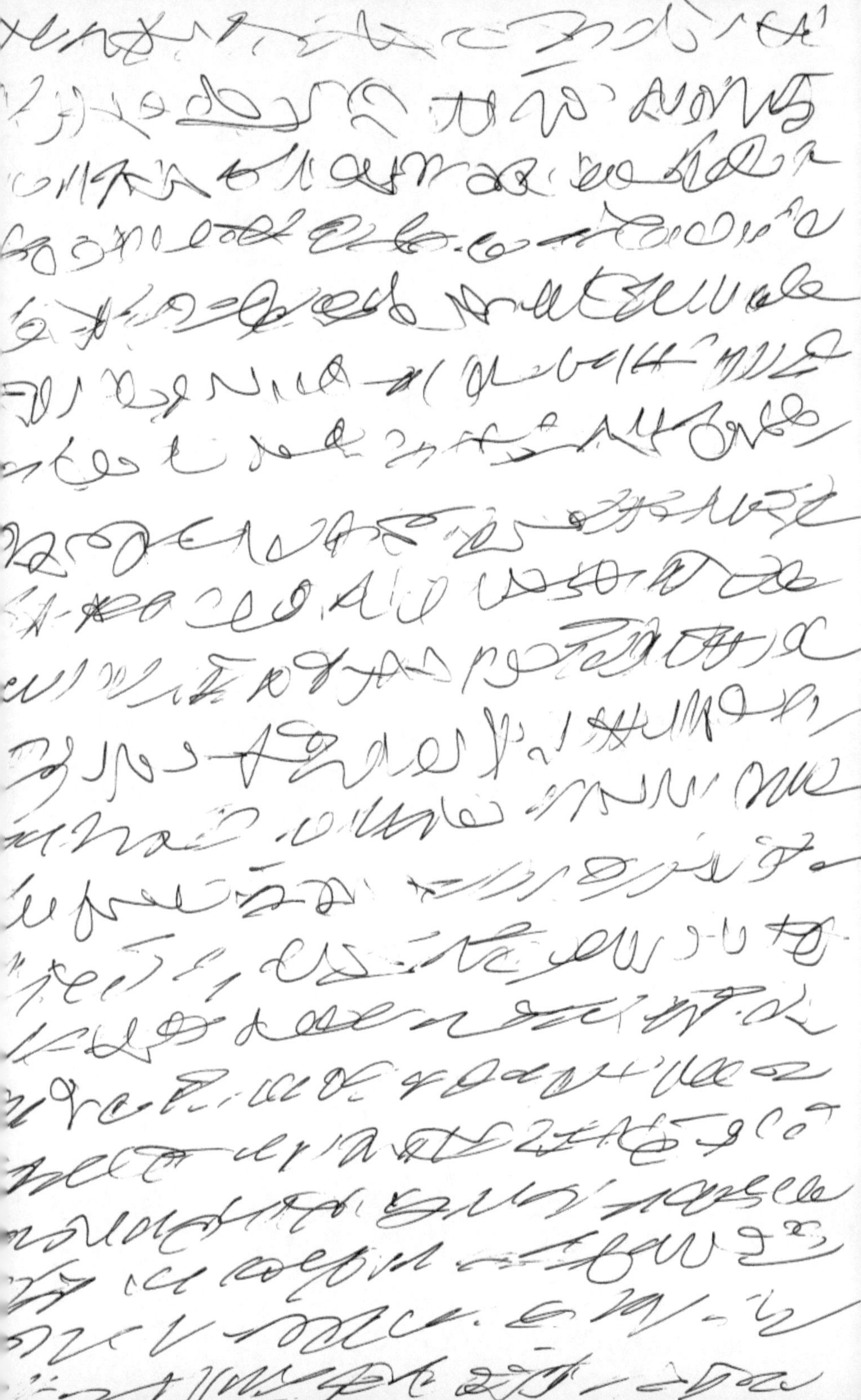

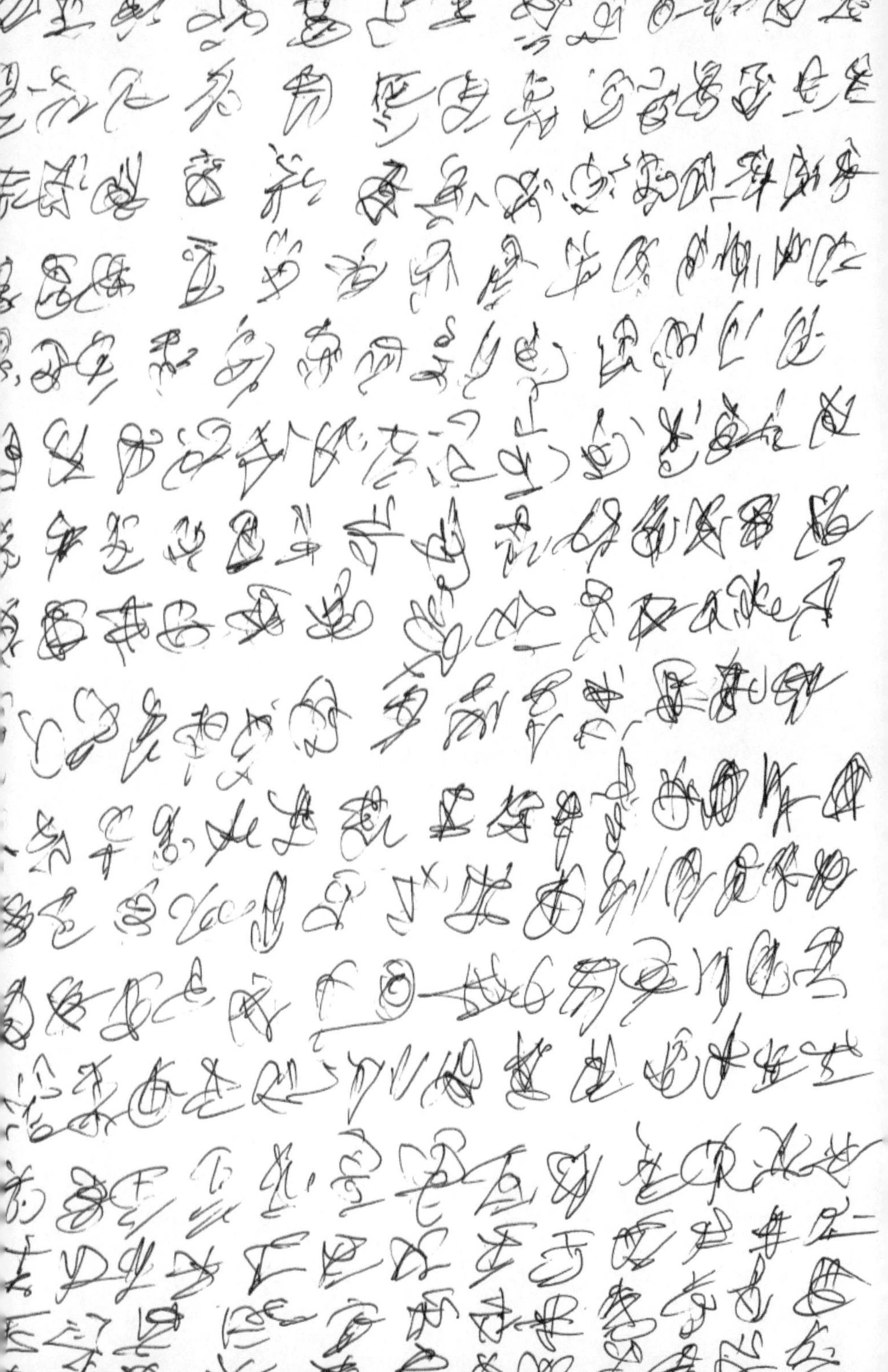

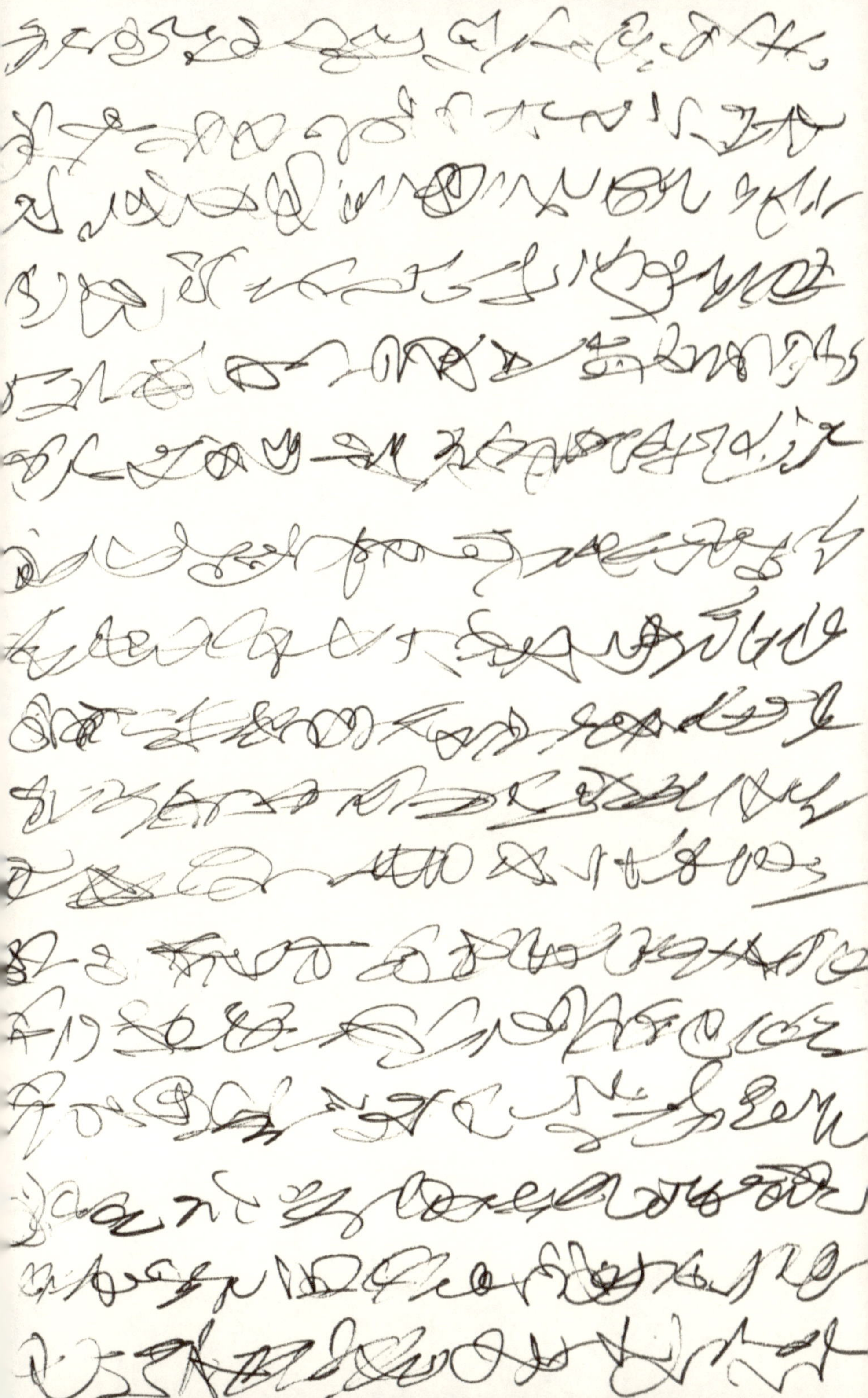

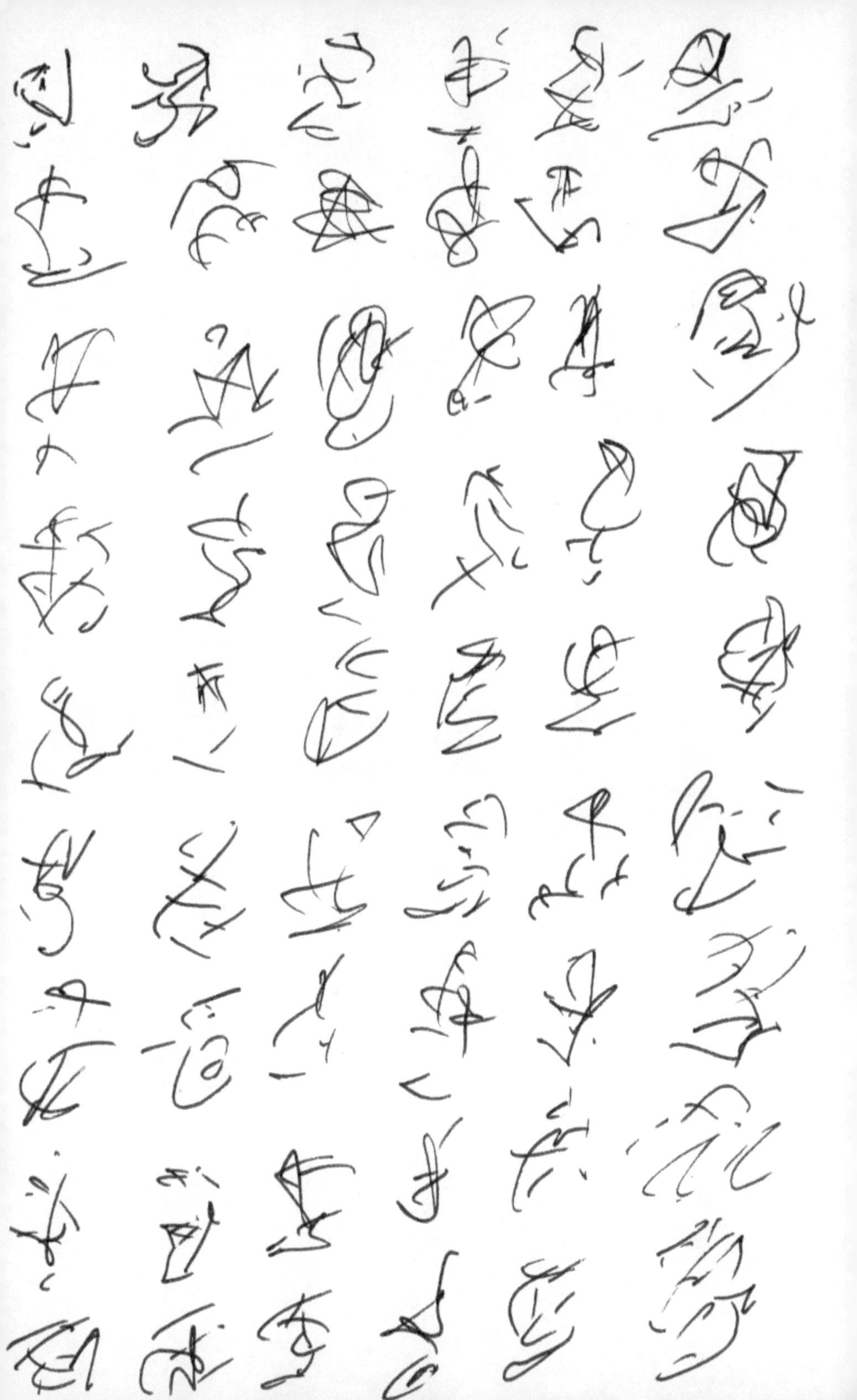

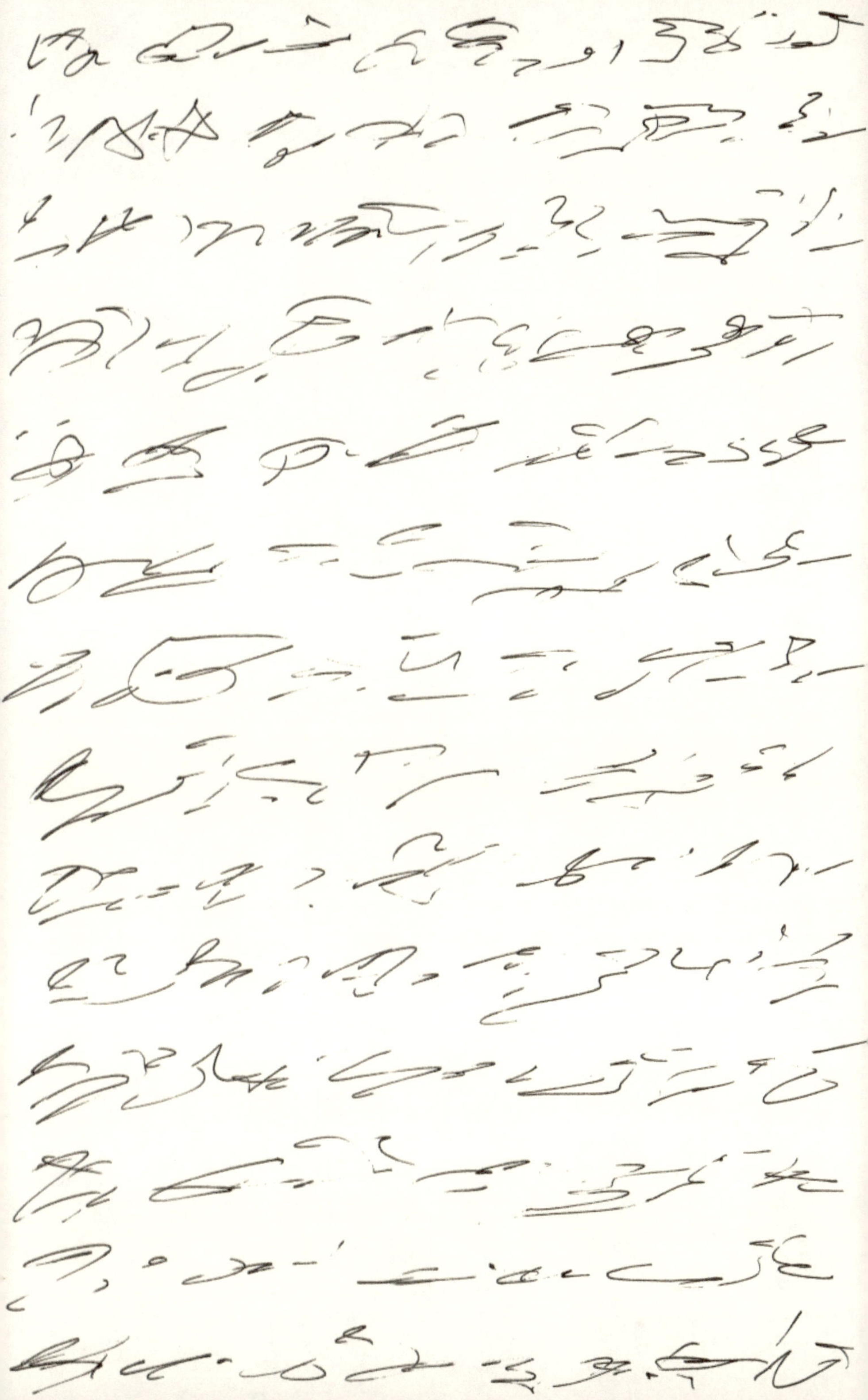

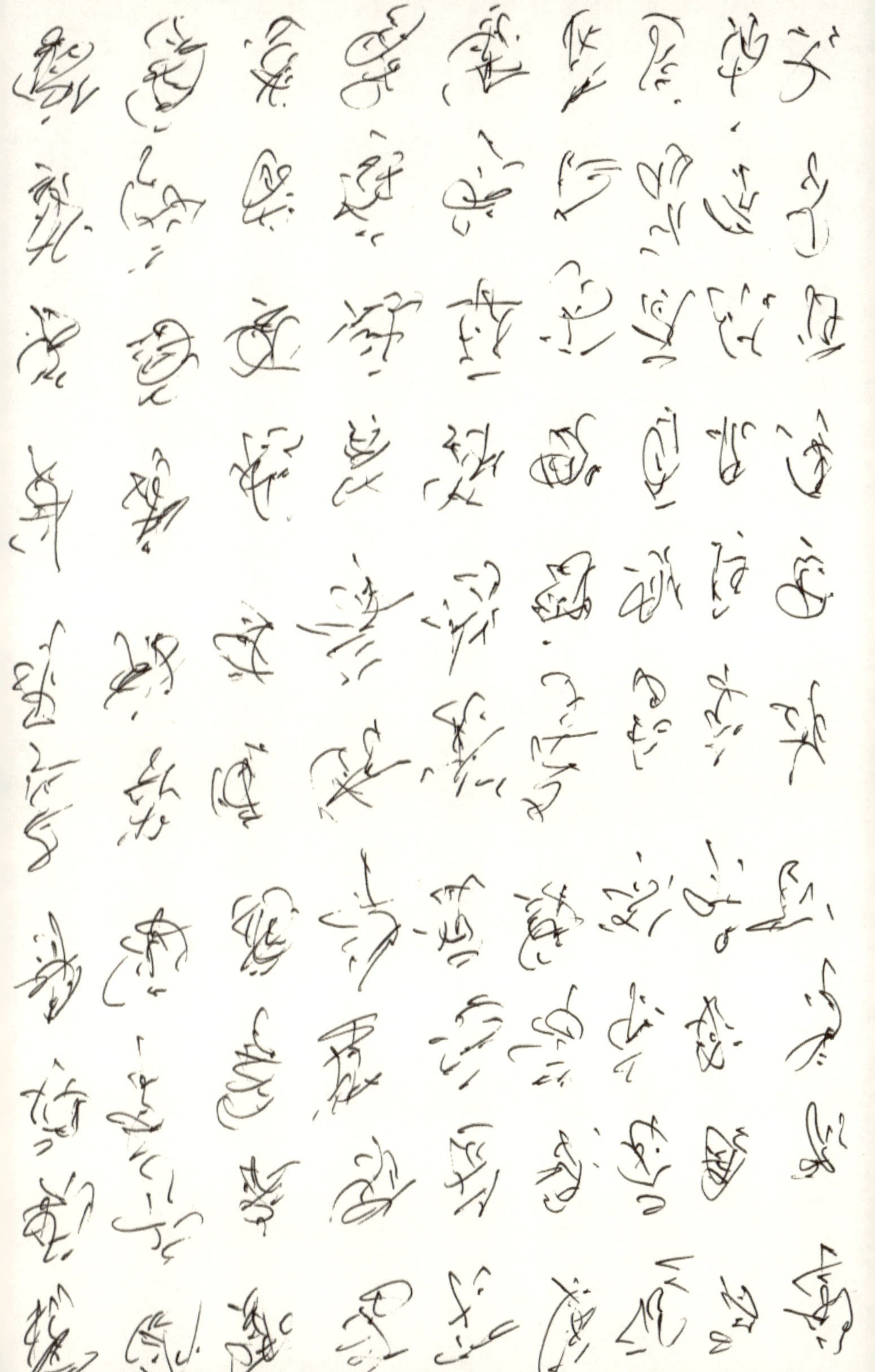

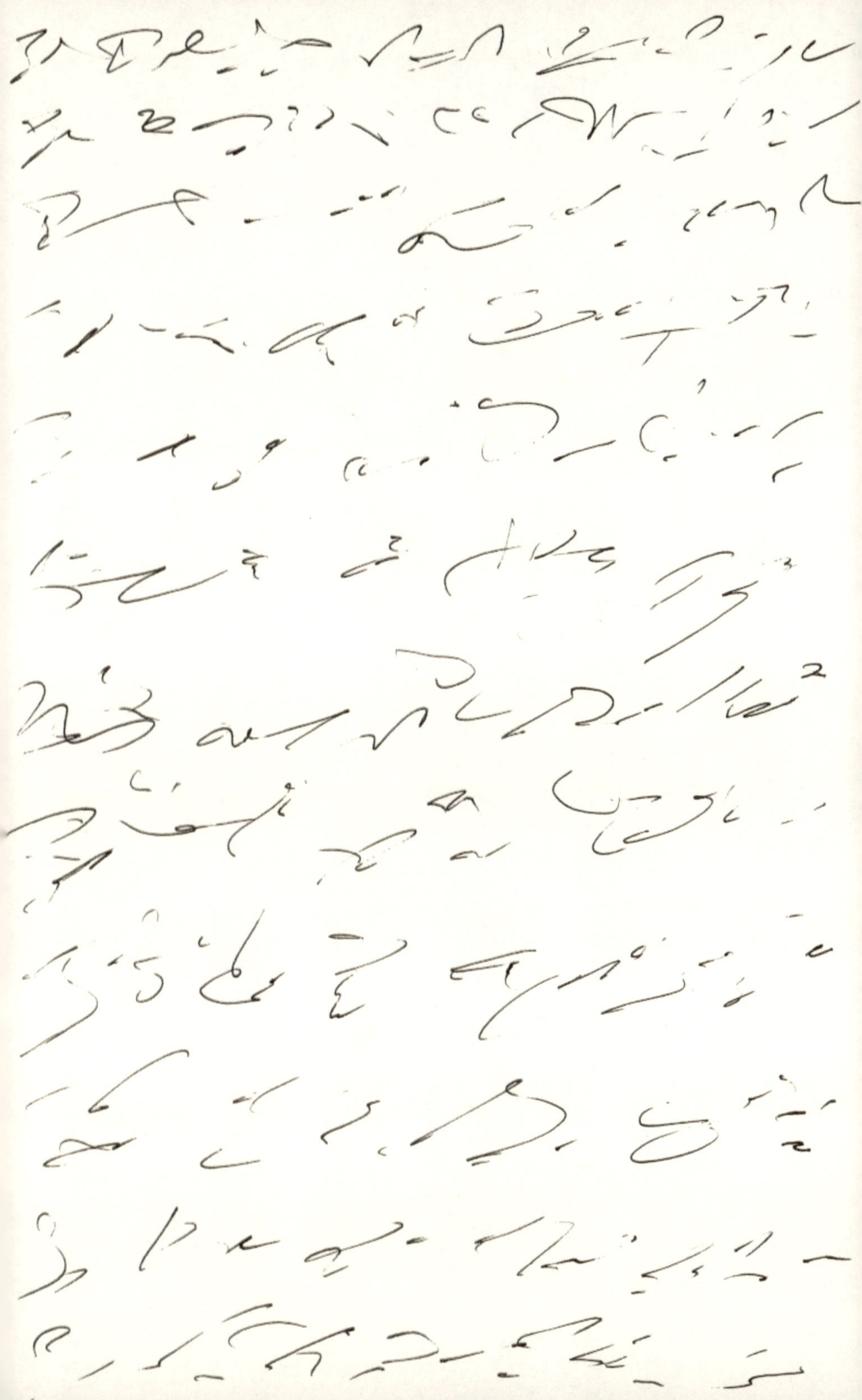

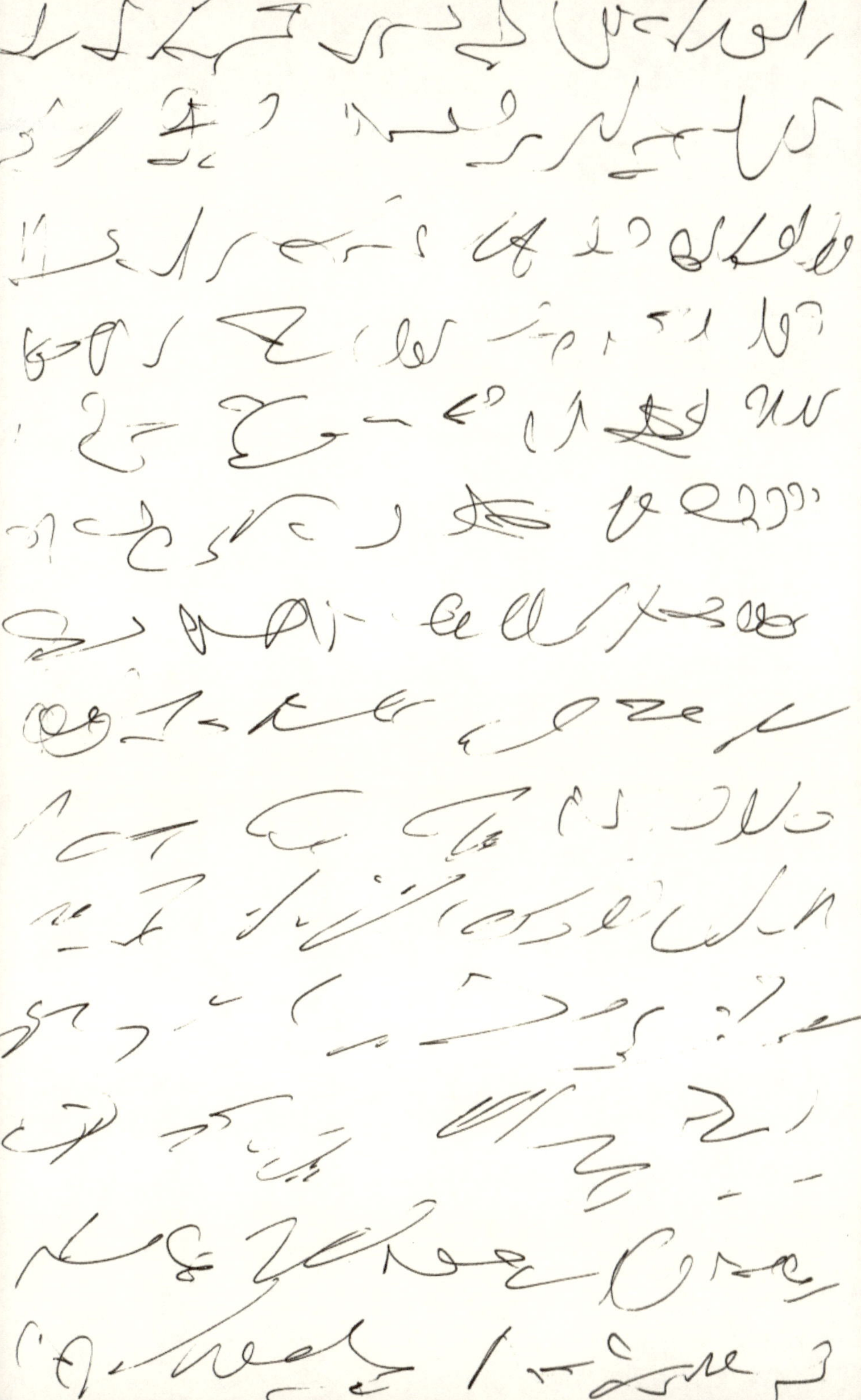

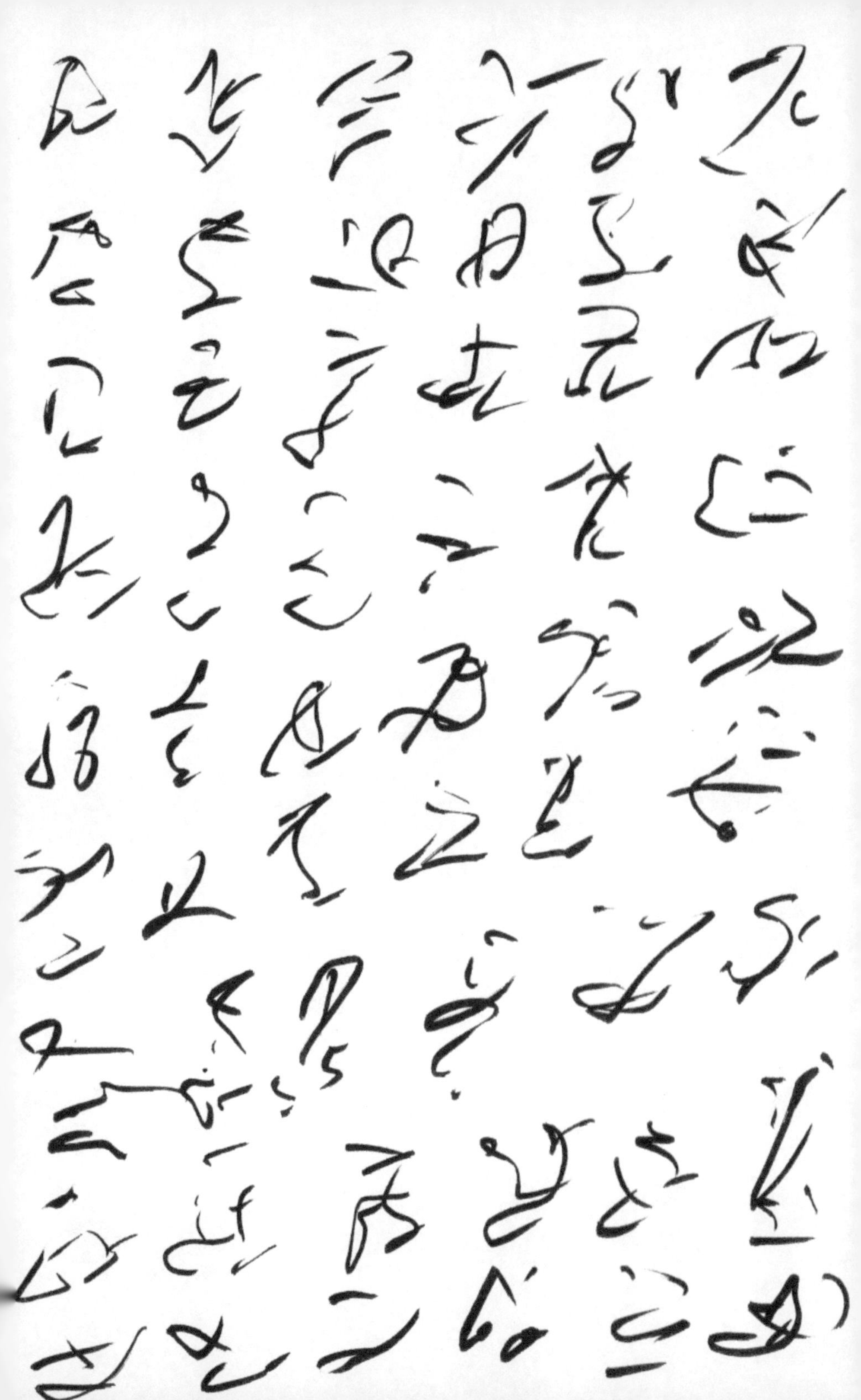

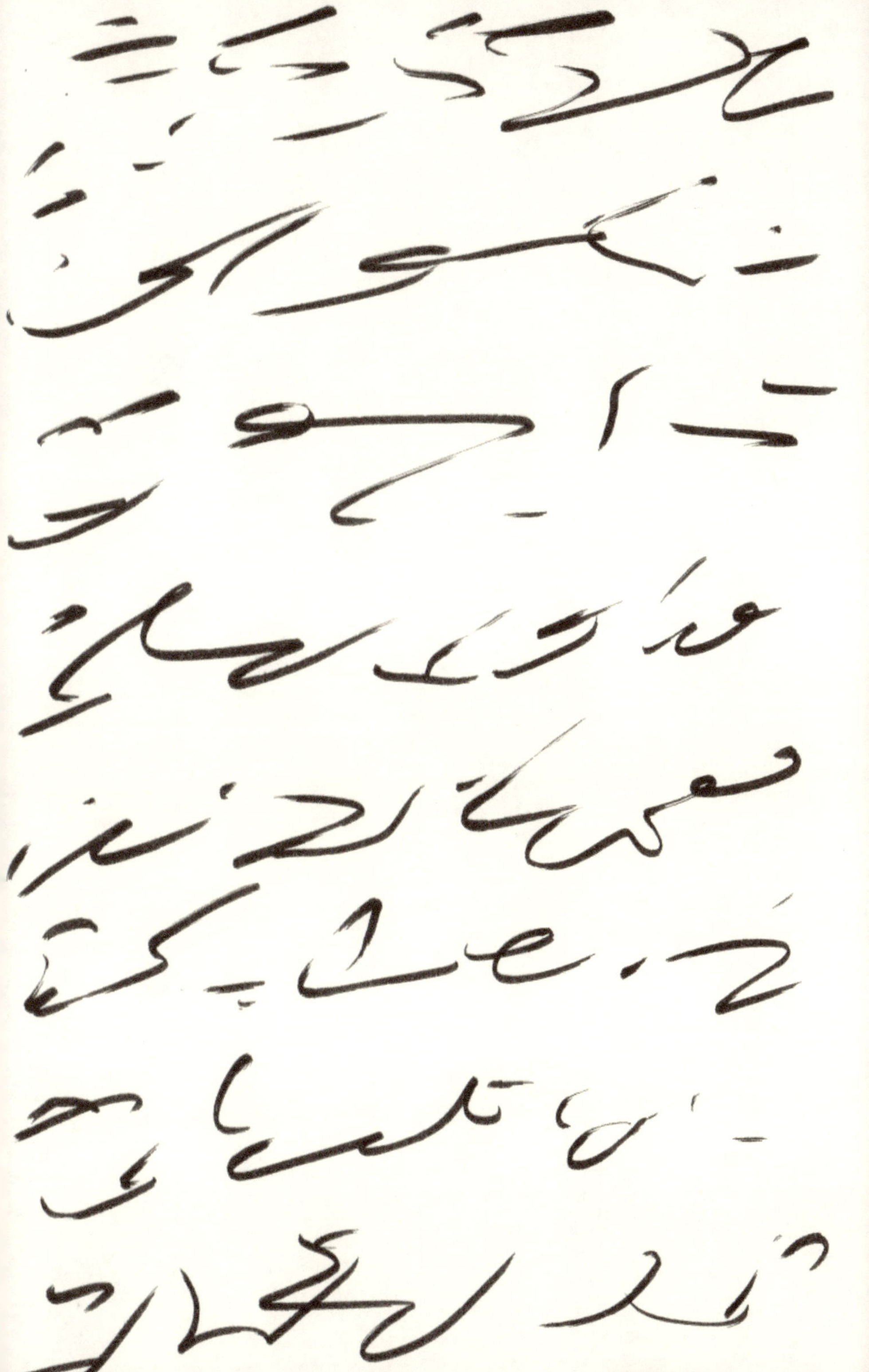

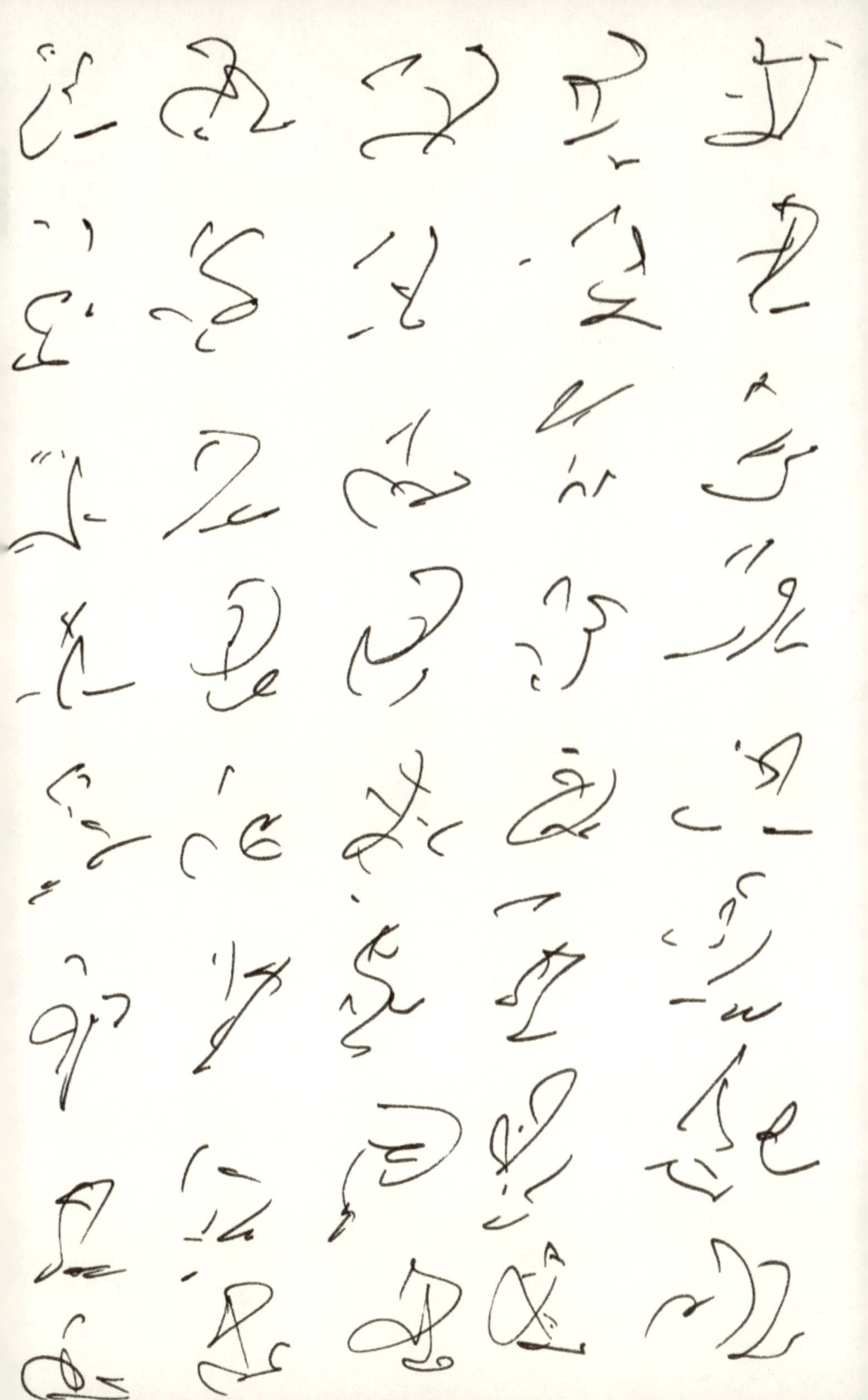

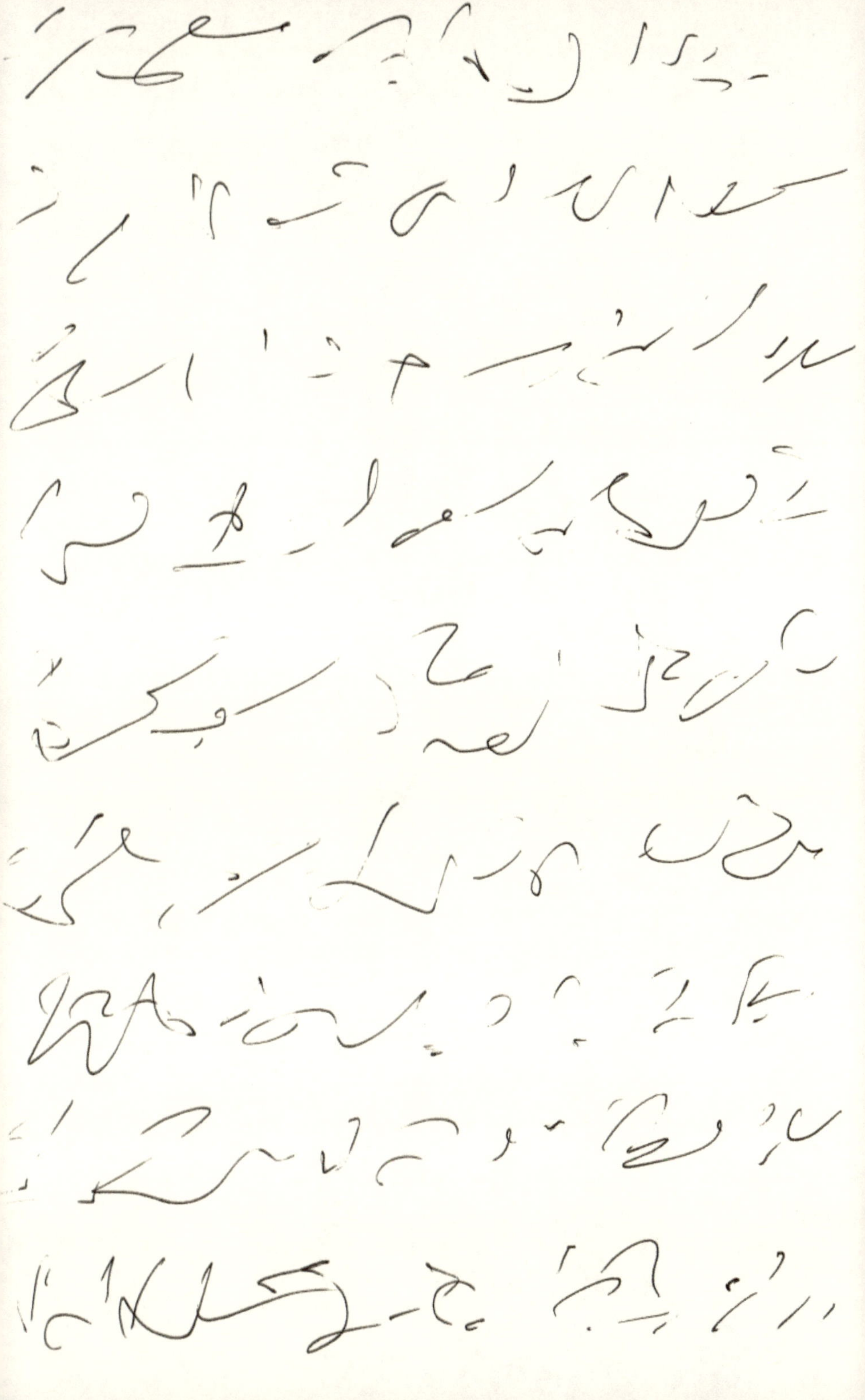

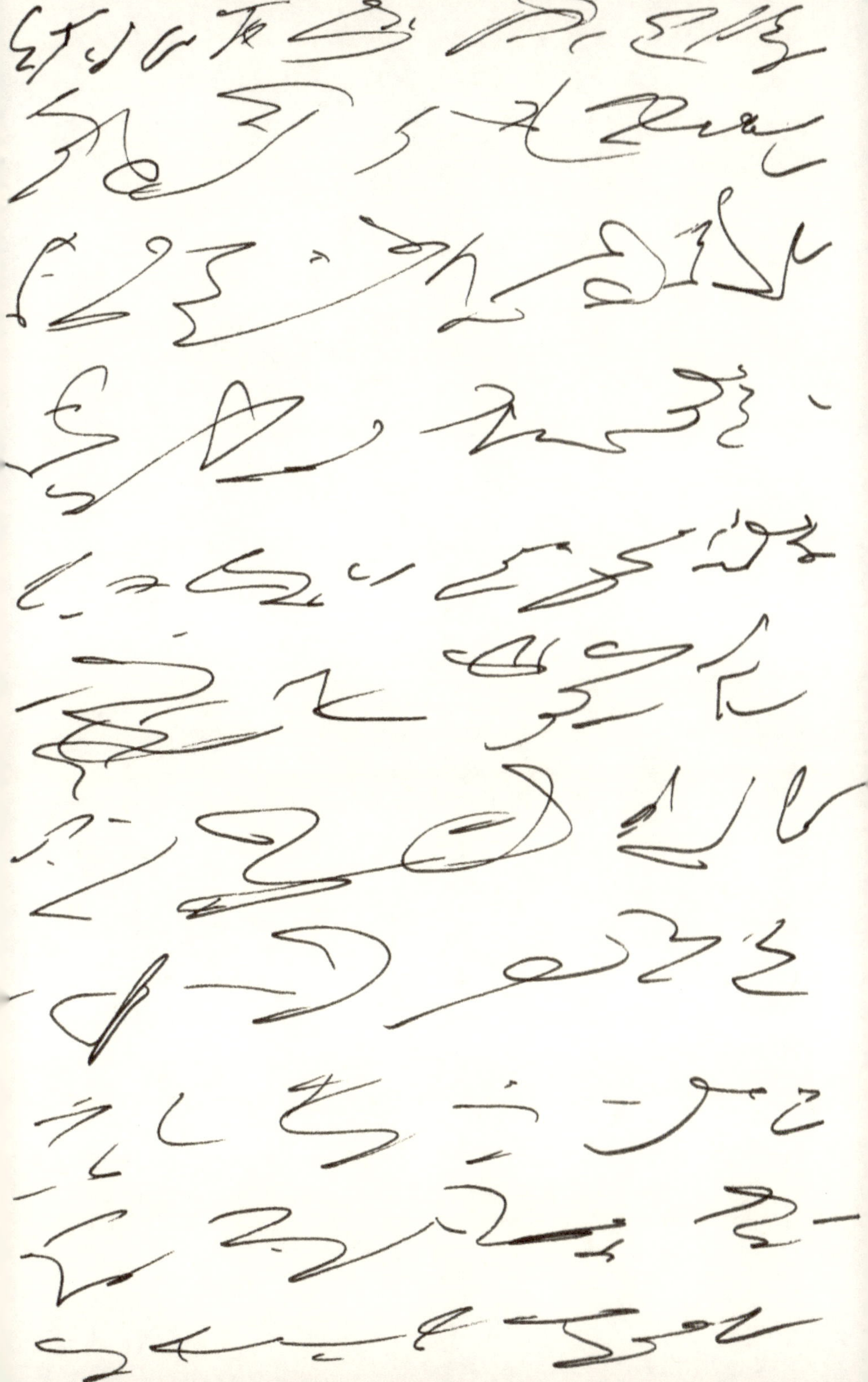

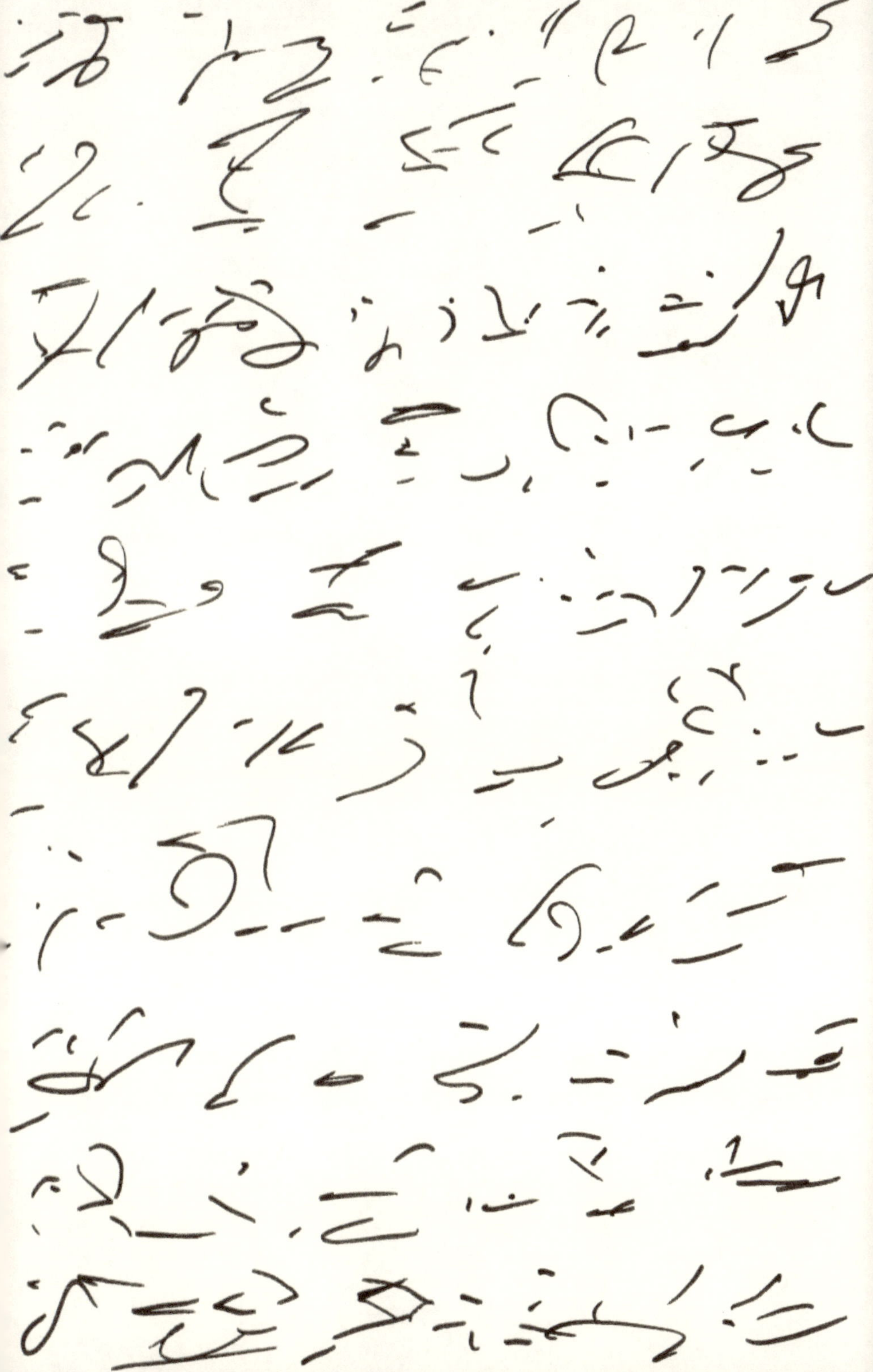

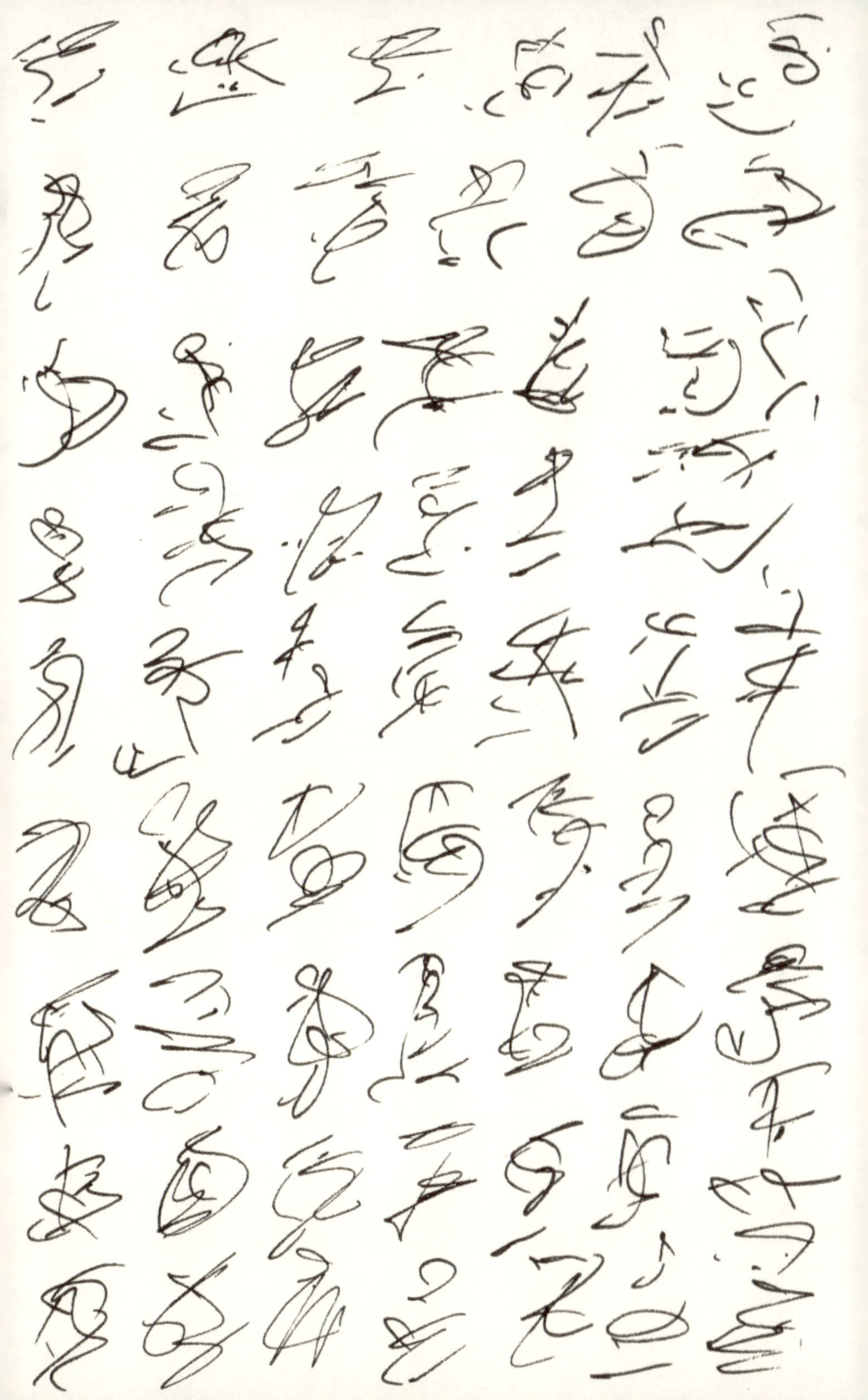

www.ingramcontent.com/pod-product-compliance
Lightning Source LLC
Chambersburg PA
CBHW030418310726
48979CB00007B/1096

* 9 7 8 1 4 2 1 8 8 6 8 0 0 *